The Pen Tap Orchestra

An Anthology

BY THE FIRST STORY GROUP
AT PIMLICO ACADEMY

EDITED AND INTRODUCED BY ROLAND CHAMBERS | 2017

FIRST STORY

Changing lives through writing

FIRST STORY

First Story changes lives through writing.

We believe that writing can transform lives, and that there is dignity and power in every young person's story.

First Story brings talented, professional writers into secondary schools serving low-income communities to work with teachers and students to foster creativity and communication skills. By helping students find their voices through intensive, fun programmes, First Story raises aspirations and gives students the skills and confidence to achieve them.

For more information and details of how to support First Story, see www.firststory.org.uk or contact us at info@firststory.org.uk.

The Pen Tap Orchestra
ISBN 978-0-85748-270-9

Published by First Story Limited
www.firststory.org.uk
Omnibus Business Centre,
39–41 North Road
London
N7 9DP

Copyright © First Story 2017

Typesetting: Avon DataSet Ltd
Cover Designer: James Hunter
Printed in the UK by Aquatint

First Story is a registered charity number 1122939 and a private company limited by guarantee
incorporated in England with number 06487410. First Story is a business name of First Story Limited.

'We all have a voice. Some never discover it. We all have stories to tell. Some never tell them. First Story has helped all these young writers to discover their writing voice, and in so doing has helped them discover themselves.'
Michael Morpurgo (author of *War Horse*)

'First Story is a fantastic idea. Creative writing can change people's lives: I've seen it happen. It's more than learning a skill. It's about learning that you, your family, your culture and your view of the world are rich and interesting and important, whoever you happen to be. Teenagers are under increasing pressure to tailor their work to exams, and to value themselves in terms of the results. First Story offers young people something else, a chance to find their voices.'
Mark Haddon (author of *The Curious Incident of the Dog in the Night-Time*)

'First Story not only does an invaluable thing for the young and under-heard people of England, it does it exceptionally well. Their books are expertly edited and beautifully produced. The students featured within are wonderfully open and candid about their lives, and this is a credit to First Story, whose teachers thoroughly respect, and profoundly amplify, their voices. The only problem with First Story is that they're not everywhere – yet. Every young person deserves the benefit of working with them.'
Dave Eggers (author of *A Heartbreaking Work of Staggering Genius*)

'First Story is an inspiring initiative. Having attended a school with a lot of talented kids who didn't always have the opportunity to express that talent, I know what it would have meant to us to have real-life writers dropping by and taking our stories seriously. And what an opportunity for writers, too, to meet some of the most creative and enthusiastic young people in this country! It's a joyful project that deserves as much support as we can give it.'
Zadie Smith (winner of the Orange Prize for fiction and author of *White Teeth*)

As Patron of First Story I am delighted that it continues to foster and inspire the creativity and talent of young people in secondary schools serving low-income communities.

I firmly believe that nurturing a passion for reading and writing is vital to the health of our country. I am therefore greatly encouraged to know that young people in this school – and across the country – have been meeting each week throughout the year in order to write together.

I send my warmest congratulations to everybody who is published in this anthology.

Camilla

HRH The Duchess of Cornwall

Thank You

Kate Kunac-Tabinor, **Maria Pop**, **Chris Scotcher** and all the designers at **OUP** for their overwhelming support for First Story, and **James Hunter** specifically for giving his time to design this anthology.

Melanie Curtis at **Avon DataSet** for her overwhelming support for First Story and for giving her time in typesetting this anthology.

Sophia Morris-Jones for her meticulous copy-editing and her enthusiastic support for the project.

Moya Birchall at **Aquatint** for printing this anthology at a discounted rate.

HRH The Duchess of Cornwall, Patron of First Story.

Thanks to:
Allen & Overy Foundation, Arts Council England, Jane and Peter Aitken, Tim Bevan and Amy Gadney, Arvon, Blackwells, Brunswick, Cheltenham Festivals, Clifford Chance Foundation, Beth and

Michele Colocci, Ernest Cook Trust, Danego Charitable Trust, Cathy and Richard Dobbs, Robert Gavron Charitable Trust, the First Story Events Committee, the First Story First Editions Club, Frontier Economics, Give A Book, Goldman Sachs Gives, Kate Kunac-Tabinor, Lake House Charitable Foundation, Letters Live, London Book Fair, John Lyon's Charity, Peter Minet Trust, Andrea Minton Beddoes and Simon Gray, Old Possum's Practical Trust, Open Gate Trust, Oxford University Press, Penguin Random House, Psycle Interactive, Laurel and John Rafter, Richard Reed, Rothschild Foundation, Sands Family Trust, Sigrid Rausing Trust, Royal Society of Literature, Sir Halley Stewart Trust, TD Securities, Teach First, Betsy Tobin and Peter Sands, Stonegarth Fund, Robin and Liselotte Vince, Garfield Weston Foundation, our group of regular donors, and all those donors who have chosen to remain anonymous.

Most importantly we would like to thank the students, teachers and writers who have worked so hard to make First Story a success this year, as well as the many individuals and organisations (including those who we may have omitted to name) who have given their generous time, support and advice.

Contents

Introduction

Roland Chambers

WRITER-IN-RESIDENCE

I've been leading First Story's creative writing programme at Pimlico since 2010, and I'm feeling sentimental because this is my last year. Next year some other writer will sit in my place, and while I know that my students will benefit from fresh ideas and a different voice, the question is will this imposter *deserve* them?

Because look at what we have here! *The Pen Tap Orchestra* is a work of genius, but not just one genius, a class of studiously scribbling maestros. Every Tuesday they congregate, some friendly nonsense is exchanged, and then they're off. The title of this anthology recalls the sound of their biros attacking the furniture. Twenty minutes later, each individual smarty-pants reads what they have written out loud to the group, and our minds are filled with fireworks or birdsong. Each piece is different. Each strikes a different note. The cumulative effect is exhilarating and humbling, and by a quarter past four we're done. We wander out of the room, like a matinee crowd stumbling out of the Wigmore Hall, baffled by so much beauty.

I can't take all the credit for this. Kira Roberts and Laura Davies led the workshops with me and contributed their ideas. Several of the exercises were borrowed from other teachers (thank you Matt Revel) and authors, including the very brilliant Caroline Bird. First Story has become a deep fund of ideas for writers to experiment with, and I know my own writing has benefitted from these weekly meetings with my students and from the many tips and tricks I have gleaned from colleagues also teaching on the programme. But the question is, have any of these so-and-sos earned the right to take over *my* spot? My kids. My particular beauties. The ones in this book. This collection of marvels. This tree of singing birds. And the answer, of course is, 'No, sir.' Not a bit of it. Not on your nelly. Never, never, never.

Not yet.

Foreword

Kira Roberts

I've now worked with First Story at Pimlico Academy for a number of years. Each year it is different. Each session is unique. Nothing beats the excitement of coming into the classroom on a Tuesday afternoon to meet a bunch of mad, creative, eager students who love to write. Every session I am pleasantly surprised by a new voice, a new slant, a new story. They never cease to amaze me with their bravery and skill. They are young authors and we are so lucky to play a small part in their journeys. Special thanks to all the assistance from the First Story team, especially Jay, Emily and Stephanie who are amazing individuals. Also to Laura Davies and Matthew Revel who keep me sane. However, above all, thank you Roland Chambers for all your hard work at the school. We are so sad to see you go after this year. The students, and I, will miss you deeply.

Pimlico Academy First Story Group

Automatic Poem — 7th February 2017

Love is the abominable abyss that awaits us all
Death is the opposite of nothingness
A razor is a book that tells you what words mean
Children: *boompa-te-boompa-te-boom!*

Madalena Marcal Whittles

Six-Word Autobiography

You don't need to know everything...

My Brother is Jack the Ripper

My brother is Jack the Ripper.
He sneaks out at night, and nobody sees him; nobody sees him but me.
I don't tell our parents, because that is mean, and I don't want to be his next victim.
That doesn't stop him from threatening me, so I try to stay out of his way.
He gives the impression that he's a nice guy, so you won't find out his secret.
One day I'll come home to find my parents dead (my brother said they were annoying him).
I tell you, I fear for my life, too.

Pigeon's Point of View

I run frantically across the streets of London. Busy shoes jostle me. I try to make my way to clearer ground. The only thought in my mind is finding my mother or, you know, if there just might be a piece of food lying around, it would do no harm to take it… right? I see a patch of space where a tree stands, and try to make my way towards it, but my view is blocked by another leg, another ankle. I am surrounded by legs, all trying to get somewhere, pushing and shouting, all similar. Not like us. I start to panic again, pecking at shoes like my life depends on it (which it kind of does), but no one takes any notice. Why did I have to fall out of that tree? This city may look beautiful from high up, but down here it's a nightmare. I see a break in the crowd and push through, only to find that the ground has disappeared and I tumble. As I try to stand, a giant, black wheel spins towards me.

I try to get out of the way, but it's too late.

Mariam Abdelhadi

Six-Word Autobiography

I'm strongly in favour of colours.

My Grandpa

My Grandpa is Homer
He tells stories of long-forgotten warriors
He passes on their stories through his words
He will live until the end of time
My Grandpa is Homer
His loud voice rearranges frightful tales
From decades past
As I curl up and listen to his memories
My Grandpa is Homer
I want nothing more than to be
In one of his stories
One day… To be remembered forever.

A Slap, Backwards...

Five fingers slam away from her soft rosy-coloured cheeks. Relief flushes her face, replacing the pain that almost numbed her. Her emotions change from shock to calm. As the small hand rapidly moves away from her delicate face, her expression relaxes. Her hair accelerates towards her face, each strand bouncing in the air joyously despite the girl's situation. As the hand moves away, so does the boy, placing each foot behind the other. Air strokes his cheeks gently. Each time his foot rests on the floor, dirt from his shoe falls and settles on the surface of the ground. The sun shines, leaving a golden hue on their peaceful-looking faces. All is calm.

Tulips Under Pillows

She put tulips under all the pillows then set fire to the house. Tears clouded her vision as she got further and further away. She didn't sob but her face was red. You could almost see the flames inside her coming out. She kept her mouth shut and ran into the fields. The sharp smell of grass hit her like a bus.

'There you go. Making up lies again.'

That's what they told her and she was sick of it. Every time she heard it she would go dizzy and feel a strange sensation, like water rising in her chest. Like a crack in the wall filled with bugs. Her face was soaked in tears. She knew she was telling the truth but they didn't believe it.

Lola Stokes

Six-Word Autobiography

There is only one Charlie's Angel.

The Girl Blowing Bubbles

I loved the way she said 'balloon'. She said it as if she were blowing bubbles. She was wearing a pastel pink dress and her hair was done up like Ginger Spice's. We were talking about her little brother's birthday party; the clown had made half the kids pee themselves and she was on clean-up duty.

Before her I had given up on the idea of being close to anyone, of being alone with anyone and being able to talk without stuttering. Everyone was the same, I decided. Everyone dressed, talked and acted the same. Everyone insisted on having the same attitude. Everyone had to be into the same things. This was why I liked Penelope: she was different.

Jack the Ripper

My sister is Jack the Ripper
She enjoys wearing fancy suits and acting as though she is
    someone she is not.
She burns pasta in water and says it doesn't matter
She is violent and rarely sympathetic.

My sister is Jack the Ripper
She has dark green eyes
She decides who gets hurt and who doesn't
She tears my dolls limb from limb.

All of her plans go off without a hitch.

The Lady's Fridge

The refrigerated hair dye was almost ready. It stood red and proud on the middle shelf. She had read that red hair dye works better if it's cold. The only other thing on the shelf with the hair dye was a punnet of strawberries. She refused to have anything not red on that shelf.

Below it was a shelf of Waitrose goods due to expire in the next three days. Among them: ham, blueberries and six cheese-and-onion pies that already looked stale in their plastic packets.

In the door of the fridge stood a bottle clearly labelled in bold black felt tip; an empty carton of milk; an orange carton turned sideways.

On the bottom shelf a can of Coke Zero had accidentally been tipped on its side and had created a small lake underneath.

My Body

My body is the bed of the sea
My eyes, large clumps of coral
My tears are the shoals of fish swimming everywhere
My hair is seaweed
My cheeks contain sharks
My lips are two shells pressed together
My eyebrows, sea snails
My hands are shipwrecks with discarded Fanta bottles on the nails
I am the ocean.

Yoana Boyanova

Six-Word Autobiography

Thirteen and enjoying playing the violin.

Girls vs. Boys

I am an 18th century girl. I am perceived as weak and uneducated. My goal is to find a husband keep him and his children happy. My goal is to cook at home and clean the house. I did not go to school. You see, only boys deserve to get a good education. I recently got a job in the theatre. My eyes glistened with excitement until I realised they only wanted me on stage to look at my body. No one has spoken up about it. You see, us women have to do what they tell us in order to keep the men happy. That's why we are here. We are not here to pursue our own dreams or to do whatever we want. We are here for the sole purpose of reproduction and our husbands. Without a husband, we are seen as miserable and unimportant. That's just how it is here.

I am a 21st century girl. I am perceived as strong and intelligent. My goal is to become a professional rugby player. My goal is to find a husband or wife that makes me as happy as I make him or her. I deserve an education just as much as any boy. I was recently asked to play a match against Wales. My whole body shook as nerves and anxiety clouded my mind. Looking around the stadium, the clouds in my mind began to clear up. I was not born to make my partner happy. I was not born to cook or clean. This was what I was born for. I am independent and I am still just as happy and important as a married woman is. Even now, I still hear many nasty things that are said about women. You only like her because of her body. I'm getting girls. Of course women should earn less. All of these comments are intolerable, inconsiderate and spiteful. Society has come a long way but there is still a long way to go before we overcome this sexism. We are all humans and deserve to be treated that way.

Minnie Waddell

Six-Word Autobiography

The bunkbed I shared with her.

Minnie not Mini

Minnie does not mean mini
I am not a stereotype
Never refer to me as 'mini'
I have grown
Evolutionised
I have significantly elongated

Death Comes on Stockinged Feet: One Hundred-Word Story

I shook hands with Death. He was wearing woollen mittens and thick woollen socks, even though it was the middle of summer. He said he always felt the cold, as if he'd been chiselled from ice. He reminded me of the moon because he was always so distant. No one really knows Death well enough to describe him.

Death. His eyes were like cages shielding him from people; his hair was like a soggy mop knotted by salty tears. His mouth was like a book, full of so many sad stories. He was so silent: Death comes on stockinged feet.

My Dad is Leonardo da Vinci

My dad is Leonardo da Vinci.
He has the same brush strokes, paint pots and splash marks
The same choice of Timberlands and policeman gloves
He has the same fingermarks on pencils and the same crayon
on card
The same pens shoved in jars and moth-eaten clothes hanging
from rails.
He has the same rectangular glasses and the dust particles that
sit on them.
The same keys and doormat, kettle and cooker, light bulb
and ceiling.
The same chestnut eyes.
My dad is Leonardo da Vinci.

Ferdous Yasin

Six-Word Autobiography

Chutney is the best sauce ever!

My Ball!

The ball I lost many years ago –
Not quite so special and ever so cheap –
Was something easily replaceable,
But when I lost it my sadness was deep.

That ball, filled with memories
Caused great sorrow when it was gone
So cheap and yet, to the contrary
Was responsible for much sadness when our time was done.

The ball I played with for many a day
Left in a park (so regrettably)
How I miss its round shape
And mourn its unfortunate destiny.

And yet in spite of all this, I must move on
For the fact is, my ball is gone.

A Cycle Without Stabilisers?

You are escorted to the playground by your dad, travelling with a sense of anxiety. The narrow pavement is covered in bumps. The half-grown bushes to the right and the fence to the left remind you of an alleyway and the tension begins to build. You are welcomed into the area by your dad, holding the door for you encouragingly. You enter, the discoloured metal fence screeching as it closes, only to be greeted by the sight of your bike, shining as bright as ever, red and orange. Your dad asks if you feel okay, noticing your face turn pale as he detaches the vital stabilisers. Your stomach feels queasy, but it is settled by your dad, looking friendly in his colourful outfit (chequered hat, leather shoes, suit trousers, bright blue shirt and worn-out old jacket).

Nevertheless, the once solid-looking bike has been changed into a dangerous, unstable form of transport. From now on, the thought of a bicycle will be associated with the word 'threat'. You sit on it tentatively, preparing yourself for the worst. Your dad reassures you with that ridiculous grown-up lie that everything is going to be fine and, with great uncertainty, you set off.

Several emotions rush through you, mainly fear, but you are comforted by the knowledge that your dad is still holding on behind you, running to keep up. You peddle, struggling to balance, your legs wobbling as you gain more speed, and you gain confidence as you look at your bike, red as ever, reflecting the light of the sun.

'Dad!' you call, and are about to say let go, but, to your surprise, he isn't behind you – no! In fact, he's quite a distance away grinning at the sight of his four-year-old son, riding his bike with no stabilisers.

Eagle

The sun blinded me with its stare as did the extreme blue of the sky. There were no clouds to shield me from the warmth it brought. I fished out my breakfast, something to keep me going for the big day ahead, and browsed my wardrobe. The uniform I was forced to wear restricted my freedom and prevented me from being as bold and tall as I usually was. I flew to my new school, looking down at the people below. I made my way from my habitat, a decaying old house with brown bricks and a half-tiled roof, the broken windows leaving shards of glass on the pavement below. Suddenly, I came to see a structure almost as high as I was with contrastingly new windows and newly painted brick walls along with a fully tiled roof. Of course, the building was a few miles away! Nevertheless I saw it. The small figures I was gliding over entertained me on my journey. Once I arrived I was greeted by the respect of the entire school, and those that approached me were dazzled by my beauty. It should be noted they did not say this to my face. I heard them say it from across the room.

Asma Deris

Six-Word Autobiography

A rose in the desert sand.

You Are

You are the opener of my eyes, mind and heart

You are the greatest teacher I could ever dream of

You are incredible, a pure inspiration

You are the maker of that magnificent odour that pulls me like a magnet to the kitchen

You are the maker of the foods that create a sensation in my mouth and stomach

You are the Tardis that takes me to another world when my heart is filled with sorrow

You are the solution to every problem; I come to you whenever I am in trouble

You are the feeling of comfort, assurance and most importantly, of love

You are the essence of my life

You are my mother, my beating heart

My Brother is Leonardo da Vinci

My brother is Leonardo da Vinci,
the greatest genius of all time – greater than Albert Einstein or
  Isaac Newton.
Da Vinci, inventor of instruments, weapons, robots, machinery,
  gadgets and even wings.
I'm glad to be his sister.

My brother is Leonardo da Vinci,
A war hero saving or slaying hundreds, inventor of the tank.
I'm glad to be the sister of a hero.

My brother is Leonardo da Vinci, painting the world's greatest
  painting –
sculpting a sculpture, designing a great design.
I'm glad to be his sister because he takes me to famous places,
  to meet famous people, to see great things: my brother.

My brother is Leonardo da Vinci, someone who protects me,
a helper of those in need, those that are innocent.
I want to be a doctor curing people of pain and disease,
Da Vinci was the greatest dreamer who ever lived.
My brother is Leonardo da Vinci.

The Dress

You walk holding your mother's hand. It is so secure and locked. Your brother goes off wandering the rest of the mall but you, of course, stay with your mother.

Something catches at the corner of your eye – a silken, cherry-red dress with golden glittery rims and twilight blue ribbon across the waist. Your size and not puffy.

The dress is the positive and you are the negative. It attracts you.

You pull on your mother's warm hand and in that sweet voice you use when you want something, you request to buy it, this mirage dress.

Reluctantly, your mother says no. Not now. Perhaps when you return that way. Later.

She is your mother and you agree.

You continue walking with a knotted string, tied to your mother. But the magnetic field that was formed thirty steps back is growing stronger.

The knot is untied as your mother takes money out of her bag, and you are drawn to the dress. You drift away.

The dress is now in front of you and there is glitter in your pupils. You go in by the shop door. You take the dress from the hanger that is the twin of the dress you saw.

You tell the owner that you would like to wear it. He asks where your mother is, but you don't know. You think only of the dress. He is looking over your head, searching for her, worried, but you keep nagging, and finally he agrees.

You put the dress on. Oh the joy! Then come out of the dressing room wanting to show your mother, wherever she is. You look for her.

And there she is. The owner is giving her a cup of water. Reassuring her. Her face has triple tears and is a cherry-red colour: almost as red as your dress. Your guilt is suddenly formed. Its size is bigger than your dress.

Scarlett Stokes

Six-Word Autobiography

Just able to stop myself imploding.

On the Merits of Me:
An Introduction

I have many names, not unlike the wind, into which my titles have been shouted many times, curses or blessings, prayers or pleas.

'Scarlett!' they cry, callous four-year-old slayer of the innocent ladybug, warrior of the trampoline-battle, prey to the fence that lay under the climbing tree in anticipation of an impaling.

I am the usurper of front car seats, traitor who spent another's gift card, squirrel lover, snake strangler, burier of baby birds. I am the liberator of hay-trapped mice, sometimes negligent carer to the Griffin – diplomat, tyrant, and, above all, a bit of a handful.

The Hound and the Fox

The mangy thing in the hound's jaws is limp, but at a twist of the killer's head and a vigorous shaking of the empty body, the victim is brought thrashing to life. Dirt-mottled clumps of fur which had lain defeated on the hoof-churned ground are drawn back to the puckered skin, sewn into each plucked hollow, dirt stripped from the strands of hair, now a nice autumnal orange. The fox writhes, going taut and slack like a rope attached to a loose sail in the wind. But then the hound recoils, jaws unclenching from the creature's spine, bloodied teeth whitening to a snarl, then a grimace, then a thought. The hound leaps back a few paces, and the fox turns quickly away, its startled face sinking into the thoughtful mask of the hunted, lowering onto its fibrous hindquarters, eyes glinting, narrowed, alert. The hound has backed off a way now, through the foliage, paws finding small nooks and holes in the leafy roadside terrain. It still eyes the fox, but the fox pays it no heed as it retreats slowly into the ferns and away from danger.

Adventures in the Wet

You walk home in the rain, scuffing a pebble ahead of you. You miss your mark, the chipped yellow line, and the rock skips down between the stiff rusted arms of a grate. But it's raining too loudly to hear whether the drain is filled with water, so you don't pause to listen. You keep walking, head trained on boots searching pebbles, the hood of your jumper sodden. Rain drips between your eyes. You blink away tears, not raising a hand. You wonder to yourself, what will you do when you find out it was all a dream?

A Beast of a Brother

My brother is a sea god,
He sits on a driftwood throne,
Draped in Wyvern pelts,
Slain and slung over the great under-sea furnaces,
To melt away the fat,
Their scales now salt-sprayed, soot-stained,
Glaring and guttural,
Hate cold as the shifting plaques on the sinuous skin.

My brother is a sea god,
He holds the sand-grass in his thrall,
On the sea shores, on the dunes,
They bend to him,
And in the briefest of breezes,
They flutter,
Strained and stiff fronds kneeling to bow.

My brother is a sea god,
He wears the rubber of weed-skin,
Anemones swirl his arms,
Urchin quills dot his brow,
Spikes shifting in the current,
An off-kilter, drifting crown.

My brother is a sea god,
From his scalp pokes
Feathers of the Ospreys and Sea Eagles,
Taken from the wings of his soldiers' fallen
In battle with the other oceans,

So when shone in,
The light that first breaks after a storm,
They become like
Melted copper on his head.

My brother is a sea god,
His eyes forged from the darkest caves,
Which hatch the brightest light,
So like bulbs of glass they glow,
Spitting yellow crab blood,
His gaze sweeping the tides,
The seas play under his eye.

My brother is a sea god,
His hands webbed and spined,
Nails shards of flint,
With webbing between each long finger,
Binding with a grainy,
Sand-filled membrane.

My brother is a sea god,
Down his back trawls
A three-set of ridged fins,
Each shoulder adorned from
Top to hand,
And one lining
The length of his undulating spine.

My brother is a sea god,
His body embellished with
Opaque scales slotted
Like armour plates,

Or shivering sands,
That when glanced into,
Not the face of the onlooker,
But that of the sister,
Sacrificed and slain,
Stares in contempt,
Back.

Romina Aghaie

Six-Word Autobiography

I am sorry but I am a rebel.

The Hare and the Tortoise: A Race in Reverse

At the start, the tortoise jumps down and up with joy, while the tired hare looks glum. During the race, a bead of sweat is sucked back into the tortoise's skin, and those standing close by can hear him exhale and inhale as he passes the slowly waking hare. Finally the tortoise crosses the finishing line with the hare far behind. The moral? Whether you tell this story backwards or forwards, slow and steady wins the race.

Hyder Al Dami

Six-Word Autobiography

I'm hilarious for a rookie comedian.

The Baron's Bedroom

You've never seen a more curious nor elegant bedroom until you have set foot in the bedroom of the sixth and greatest Baron Byron. Be assured that you will walk away in awe and astonishment; in happiness and in merriment; in darkness and in gloom. Strangers are often not even permitted to enter the Baron's room lest they be tortured by the sounds of the Baron's bagpipes.

Even his bed is grand and majestic causing a fellow stranger to cry, 'Oh, he is not the Baron but an emperor of glory and riches!' Yet a Baron he is. Even the walls are intimidating. He has seven wardrobes filled with exotic robes, crimson tunics, unworn dazzling boots and dangling turbans.

However, though the colours of the room dance like fire, it is really as dark as the Baron's soul. The Baron doesn't take kindly to strangers in his place of solitude and joy.

If You Take That Risk…

If you take that risk
You will tremble at the unearthly sights and feel darkness
    wrapping itself around you
You will hear a deep menacing voice and face the terror of an
    unknown tongue
You shall witness evils and feel the urge to run away, stammering
    and in tears
If you carry on, you will begin to choke as well
You will feel embarrassed and ashamed
You will be haunted for days

However, if you do not take this risk
It will be eternally damning for you to know that you did not
    take that risk.

Leila Chady

Six-Word Autobiography

Curly, candied, fun, hyper loving me.

Making a Sandwich (Backwards)

I picked up the piece of lettuce and put it into its transparent wrapper making sure to seal it tightly in order to keep it fresh. I took a slice of turkey and did the same, working gently. Opening the fridge door, I put it in its place. I took two slices of soft, wholegrain bread and returned them to the loaf.

Now, I thought, I am going to make the <u>perfect</u> Sandwich!

His Fridge

There were three shelves in *his* fridge. On the first were six cans. Some had labels that read 'Dog Food'. Inside the cans was a green liquid that contained badly chopped pig heart for his dachshund. They were large cans with half opened lids and dried blood encrusted on the sides. On the second shelf sat a plate. It was filthy and had a fox paw lying on a bed of rice with a garnish of parsley delicately placed on top. At the back of the shelf was a single lonely bottle that was glowing green. It had 'Deer Poison' written on a Post-it note taped carefully to the side.

Aaliyah Nanglegan

Six-Word Autobiography

The fantasies are in your dreams.

Bladedancer: The One Who Dances with the Blades

When the Nightmare consumes the Light,
When they're singing a broken sound,
Don't let them finish,
There is a chance you can save the Light –
Your heart,
Don't let the Blight consume you whole,
They're corrupting your dance,
But don't let this end,
Remember you told yourself, 'I can continue'.

Start anew or continue
Your light will keep growing
Your ability to shine.
Intelligence and beauty is your way
Each step, each step,
Flows in their melodies,
Flows in this dance,
Flows in the rhythm,
A single beat can cause a static blitz
It sparks your light,
Each beat, each rhythm
This boulevard of corrupted wills
These Blades are your instrument,
These Blades are your Conductor,
You dance with these Blades in your hands
These Blades:
Let's dance.

The Butterfly

As the resting trees sway east, the sun crawls to the west. A red winged butterfly drifts from bark to bark. It flies over a stream and upwards to the top of a little spouting waterfall, past cracks of mossy rocks piled together. The butterfly travels. As it passes, small specks of ants retreat to the hill while plants or flowers slowly close up their petals or retreat to fertile dirt.

The tiny red winged creature soars, then, slowly descending, its colour grows brighter in the sunlight. It flies into a small meadow, a flower patch filled with pansies, roses, tulips and a purple orchid. The butterfly descends under a leaf where a shell has opened. It creeps inside, covering its red ruby wings with the shell. It falls asleep as the cocoon sticks to the leaf, hanging over the purple orchid.

Lena Elghamry

Six-Word Autobiography

Lena: a charming yet feisty person.

Kettle

I want to be a kettle
Boiling water
For pasta
For tea

I want to be a kettle
Hot as the sun
Loud as a gun
All I want, is to be a kettle

The One Who Was Always There

As I enter the place I know best
I see you sitting on the sofa staring at your phone
I hear a deep silence
From the day I was born, your love fluttered in the air
Lavender and flowers are what I smell
I go into my room and read a large book
You walk in and I look up

Matilda Collins

Six-Word Autobiography

An ocean deep with shallow waters.

Pen

I want to be a pen
Ink flowing through me
A holder of creativity

I want to be a pen
A patch of inspiration and success with plastic casing
A way to show off one's ability

I want to be a pen
Pocket-sized, helpful and shiny
Although a friend to most, one day my ink will run out
And although I will eventually become useless
I will have belonged to the author of a short story
The artist behind a quick sketch
The mathematician who has solved a tricky problem
I want to be a pen

Suffragette

My sister's a suffragette.
Bright blue eyes full of ambition.
She's constantly powerful.
She knows what she wants.

My sister is a suffragette.
Undeniably focused – even at the worst of times

My sister's a suffragette.
Whether she's fighting for her rights
Or fighting for the right to sit in the passenger seat
My sister's a suffragette.

Elna Petros

Six-Word Autobiography

Does your talent define your future?

Questions

Am I really what I think I am? Do I really know myself as well as I should? Do I need to take a long walk down memory lane? I still wonder what gets me through the day. Is it my confidence? Is it my friends? My family? I always wonder when I play. That's what gets me through the day.

Your House

Your house smells lovely. It smells strong and sweet. I remember when you made me the best pancakes ever. They were amazing. You always have a contagious smile on your face. You're always happy. You are generous and loving.

Tala Awada

Six-Word Autobiography

Tala is sweet, generous and caring.

Picture Frame

I want to be a picture frame
Make people feel joyful when they look at me
Adore me
For who I am
They will love me
The respect I will get every day
'Wow, that is the best painting I have ever seen!'
They will sell me for millions
Everyone will stand there taking pictures,
Like it's Hollywood
I will be a sturdy picture frame
With fabulous, detailed
Designs on my frame
Different colours on my body
People will polish my sides day after day
The wonder I will get:
I want to be a picture frame.

THE PEN TAP ORCHESTRA

Bianka Nycole
Ramon Calva

Six-Word Autobiography

Fantasy is always better than reality.

One Hundred-Word Story

Once again for the camera! Each picture changes my life forever. Every one of them. Even now it's funny that I still freeze up although I should be used to it. Yet every time I am asked for a photo I can't help thinking how, in each and every one of them, a shadow seems to lurk behind me, always getting closer, catching up to me. Reminding me, threatening me. Letting me know that I have little time left. Don't they know, that every single picture they take is killing me? It's so close now. Once again for the camera.

Hugh Kindred

Six-Word Autobiography

Stories are just an ice breaker.

Changed Lives

We sit down for lunch. The first one is red in the face, screaming in anger at the second one. He lunges and takes a swing while simultaneously thumping his chest just before his fist connects, creating the illusion of contact. I jump at the sound, before realising the trick.

The second one makes a joke about the first one's height, settles his glasses on his nose, then goes back to humming the title track from the latest James Blake album.

The third one glues a picture of Rihanna to the cover of his art book, then digs into his third helping of jacket potato, grumbling about the football scores.

The fourth one tries to sit on the fifth one, while spouting off cricket facts and mosquito trivia.

The fifth one, upon being denied a share of cake for the 104th time this year, goes off on a tirade to no one in particular about the morals of internet files and the genetic and cultural superiority of the Spanish people.

The sixth one, picking the peas out of his pasta, disagrees with everyone and asks why we can't all just be giant highly weaponised robots instead, or, at least, rocket-powered cars.

Take Me (Untitled)

splendid in music, frozen in time
an instantaneous moment, lusting forever with cold
chills, that pass by leaving a trail of warm in their wake, for what?
could be more pleasant? stranded in the cold,
my cry will be heard; oh, take me to japan! for what?
they ask. my rice hot, my music mournful, my time
running out, but never finished, on a threshold. What
is the feeling? sadness, in the opposite direction. a reverse
    in time.
imagine, princes in the slum, peasants in the palace, the king is
    out cold
round and round the merry-go-round. not quite time for
    happiness.
now it's you out in the cold – and what a sound we have shared

Unwritten

I sat at my desk. The first few chapters of my new book already on the screen in front of me. I sighed. The planning had been simple. But the actual act of commencing was easier said than done. Casting my mind forward, I tried to recall the inspiration for writing the book. And then it clicked. Fingers on the keyboard, I began lifting away. The words vanished off the screen, page after page. Before I remembered it, a whole three chapters had gone by and I had already broken a sweat. Area descriptions, character introductions; all deleted under my lifting of the keys. The redemption arc, the main love interest's backstory, the tragic death of the main character's childhood best friend and probably my favourite conversation starter that I ever wrote, that actually made it to the final draft, all gone. The photographs on the fridge began to disappear. My character became blander as personality traits vanished into the ether.

Before I knew it, I had started at the beginning. The dreaded first line. I glanced up at the clock and it was already 5 am, and I hadn't had breakfast. But I had to begin. What was the first line?

'Call me Ishmael?'

'A giant turtle swam methodically through the dark expanse of the universe?'

'There is no lake at camp green lake?'

All great ideas. I removed it from the page, I could leave it for later. But what of the genre? The premise? A book or screenplay? Thoughts poured out of my mind, until it was left completely blank.

I spat my afternoon coffee into its cup.

Matt Revel

Six-Word Autobiography

I was alone. Now there's three.

23 Weeks

When you were 23 weeks grown
I planted peas
Hard to believe such dry, dimpled petals will thrust living and
    green through the earth
I raked trenches and sowed, marked rows with sticks and hoped
But I know with care life will come

When you were 23 weeks grown
I saw the plum tree blossom
It's hard to believe these dainty propellers of petals
So light on the breeze, will hang heavy and plump and mauve
    with juice
But I know warm fruit will grow

When you were 23 weeks grown
Geraniums peeped from the cold ground
It's hard to believe what shrank into soil for winter and
Hid under cracking quilts of dried leaves
Returned with clumps like reaching hands
But I know with rest, the weary return

When you were 23 weeks grown
The sun shone
Bluebells nodded their like horses' bridled heads
And we walked amongst them as leaves unfolded and light
    became gold again

The Genie in a Lantern

I rubbed the lantern's tummy,
At the end of a busy day
And listened very carefully
For what the genie had to say
At first no sounds
Then, thud, thud
Like tiny fingers drumming on a window pane
Or the fall of heavy crystal droplets, a shower of autumn rain
The genie isn't talking yet,
Can't grant my wishes when I'm blue
But because the genie's in the lantern
My wishes have come true

The Lini-Lini Lin Marine

She's the most wonderful thing I've ever seen, the Lini-Lini
    lin marine
Of cutting through water, she is the queen
The Lini-Line lin marine
She's so very fast, it's quite obscene
The Lini-Lini lin marine

It's the only place you've ever been, the Lini-Lini lin marine
You'll leave soon, but I wouldn't be keen,
To leave the warmth of the Lini-Lini lin marine
Where you don't have to cook or clean
In the Lini-Lini lin marine
But get a full menu of fine cuisine
In the Lini-Lini lin marine

And you don't have to stick to any routine in the Lini-Lini
    lin marine
But there are no windows, you can't check the scene
Outside the Lini-Lini lin marine
And maybe you'll get bored; no TV, books or magazines
In the Lini-Lini lin marine

But at night you bounce around like there is a trampoline in
In the Lini-Lini lin marine
But as you've grown, you'll feel like a tinned sardine
In the Lini-Lini lin marine
So it must be a matter of time
And barring something unforeseen
We'll welcome you smiling from the Lini-Lini lin marine